Marsupial Sue

JOHN LITHGOW

Marsupial Sue

Illustrated by

JACK E. DAVIS

Simon & Schuster Books for Young Readers

New York   London   Toronto   Sydney

Marsupial Sue,

A young kangaroo,

Hated the hopping that kangaroos do.

It rattled her brain,
It gave her migraine,
A *backache, sideache, tummyache,* too.

One morning in May
Sue wandered away,
Leaving her relatives grazing on hay.

What did she see
Way up in a tree?
Koalas, gaily at play.

And suddenly Sue was convinced she had found
A way to escape all that bouncing around.
She climbed to the top,
She heard a loud POP!
And howling in pain fell again to the ground.

Marsupial Sue,

A lesson or two:

Be happy with who you are.

Don't ever stray too far from you.

Get rid of that frown

And waltz up and down

Beneath a marsupial star.

If you're a kangaroo through and through,

Just do what kangaroos do.

With summer at hand
The weather was grand,
So Sue stole away from her kangaroo band.

Combing the shore,
She heard someone snore:
A platypus, asleep in the sand.

"How cozy!" she said,
Completely misled,
Ignoring the probable trouble ahead,

"How perfect for me!
A life by the sea!
All snug in a watery bed!"

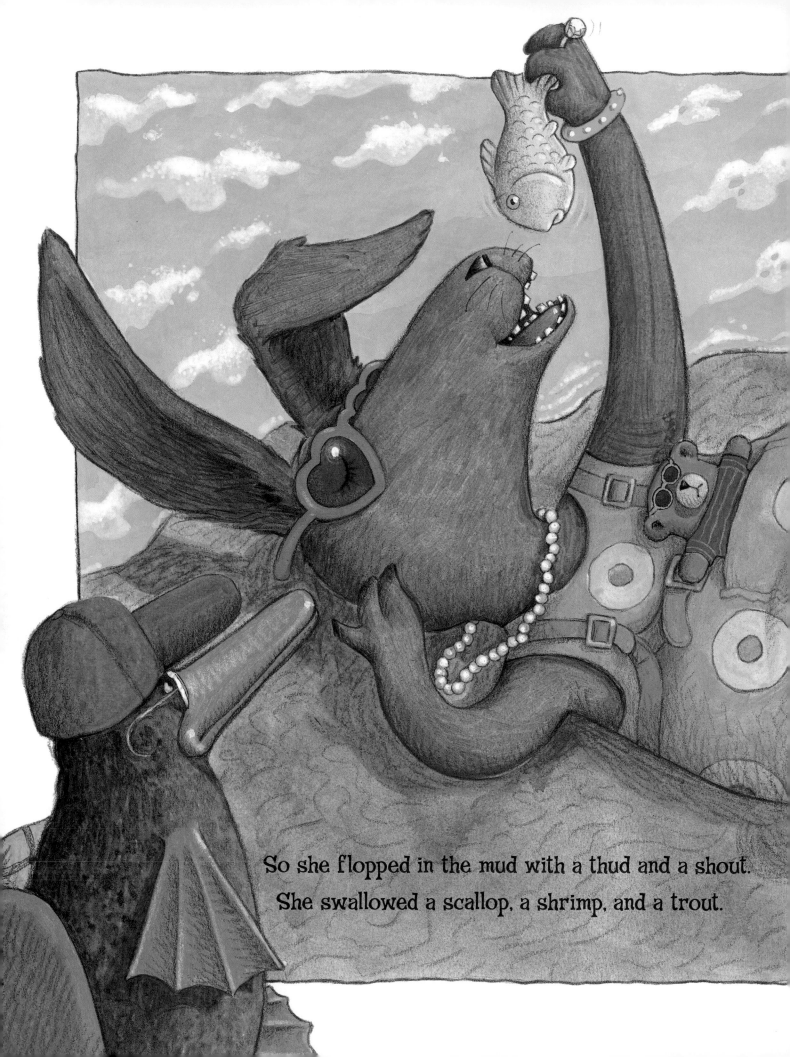

So she flopped in the mud with a thud and a shout.
She swallowed a scallop, a shrimp, and a trout.

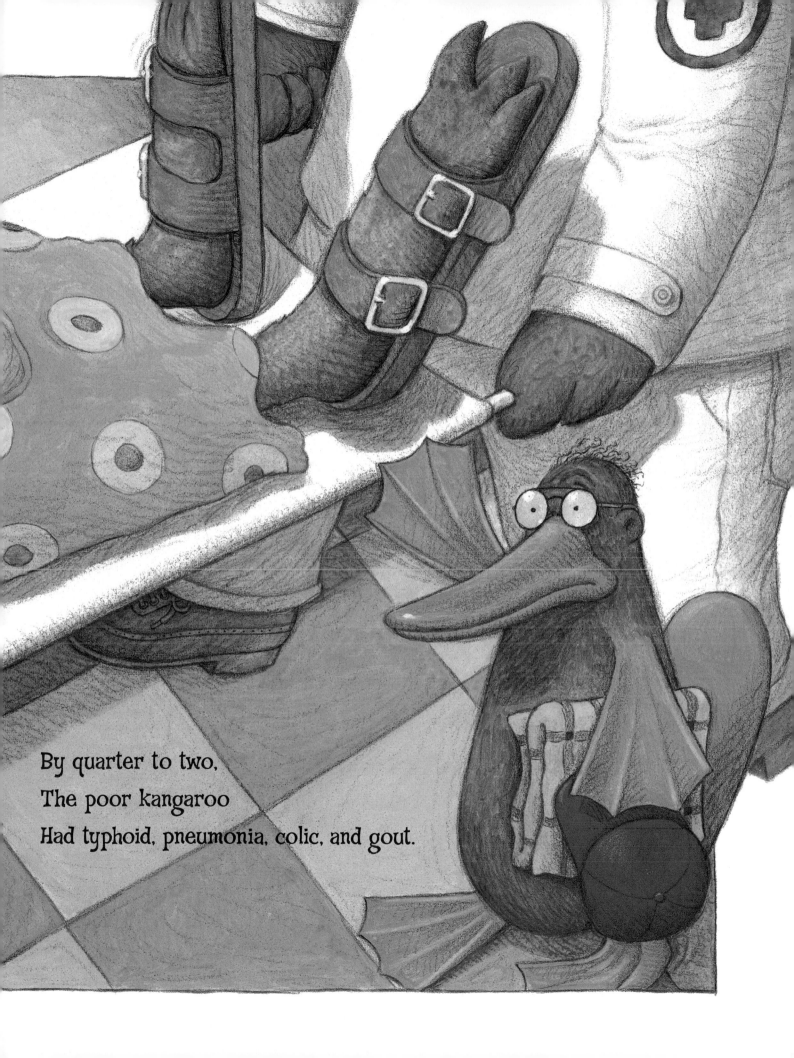

By quarter to two,
The poor kangaroo
Had typhoid, pneumonia, colic, and gout.

Marsupial Sue,

A lesson or two:

Be happy with who you are.

Don't ever stray too far from you.

Get rid of that frown

And waltz up and down

Beneath a marsupial star.

If you're a kangaroo through and through,

Just do what kangaroos do.

That autumn once more

Sue got to explore

A creature she'd never laid eyes on before.

A version of her,

In miniature—

A wallaby, with cousins galore.

Before very long,
Sue joined in the throng,
Flouncing and jouncing and bouncing along.
Happy and free,
She shouted with glee:
"At last, I'm where I belong!"

Then she looked at the wallaby, sprightly and small,

Exactly like her only not quite so tall.

She widened her eyes,

And cried with surprise,

"A kangaroo's life's not so bad after all!"

Marsupial Sue,

No longer so blue:

You're happy with who you are.

You'll never stray too far from you.

You're rid of that frown,

So waltz up and down

Beneath a marsupial star.

You are a kangaroo through and through,

So do what kangaroos do.

You are a kangaroo through and through,

So do what kangaroos do.

Marsupial Sue

lyrics: John Lithgow
music: Bill Elliott

Waltz ♩ = 210

1. Mar - su - pi - al Sue, a young kan - ga - roo, ha - ted the hop - ping that kan - ga - roos do. It rat - tled her brain, it gave her mi - graine, a back - ache, side - ache, tum - my - ache, too.

(Piano) One morn - ing in May Sue wan - dered a - way, leav - ing her rel - a - tives graz - ing on hay. What did she see way up in a tree? Ko - a - las, gai - ly at play. And sud - den - ly Sue was con - vinced she had found a

To Sarah and Arthur, my Mom and Dad
—J. L.

For Johnny, Michael, and Baby Jason
—J. E. D.

SIMON & SCHUSTER BOOKS FOR YOUNG READERS
An imprint of Simon & Schuster Children's Publishing Division
1230 Avenue of the Americas, New York, New York 10020
Text copyright © 2001 by John Lithgow. Illustrations copyright © 2001 by Jack E. Davis
"Marsupial Sue" score copyright © 2001 by Bill Elliott Music and John Lithgow
All rights for Bill Elliott Music controlled and administered by Universal Music Corp.
All rights reserved including the right of reproduction in whole or in part in any form.
SIMON & SCHUSTER BOOKS FOR YOUNG READERS is a trademark of Simon & Schuster.
Book design by Paul Zakris
The text for this book is set in 18-point Fink Roman.
The illustrations are rendered in colored pencil, acrylic, dye, and ink.
Manufactured in China
12 14 16 18 20 19 17 15 13

Library of Congress Cataloging-in-Publication Data

Lithgow, John, 1945-
Marsupial Sue / by John Lithgow ; illustrated by Jack E. Davis.
p. cm.
Summary: Marsupial Sue, a young kangaroo,
finds happiness in doing what kangaroos do.
ISBN 978-0-689-84394-5
[1. Kangaroos—Fiction. 2. Identity—Fiction.
3. Stories in rhyme.] I. Davis, Jack E., ill. II. Title.

PZ8.3.L6375 Mar 2001
[E]—dc21
00-046998
0114 SCP